PRAISE FOR M. L. BUCHMAN

Tom Clancy fans open to a strong female lead will clamor for more.

— DRONE, PUBLISHERS WEEKLY

(Miranda Chase is) one of the most compelling, addicting, fascinating characters in any genre since the Monk television series.

— DRONE, ERNEST DEMPSEY

(*Drone* is) the best military thriller I've read in a very long time. Love the female characters.

— SHELDON MCARTHUR, FOUNDER OF THE MYSTERY BOOKSTORE, LA

Superb!

— DRONE, BOOKLIST, STARRED REVIEW

A fabulous soaring thriller.

— TAKE OVER AT MIDNIGHT, MIDWEST BOOK REVIEW

Meticulously researched, hard-hitting, and suspenseful.

The first...of (a) stellar, long-running (military) romantic suspense series.

Expert technical details abound, as do realistic military missions with superb imagery that will have readers feeling as if they are right there in the midst and on the edges of their seats.

Buchman has catapulted his way to the top tier of my favorite authors.

M L. Buchman's ability to keep the reader right in the middle of the action is amazing.

The only thing you'll ask yourself is, "When does the next one come out?"

I knew the books would be good, but I didn't realize how good.

SWEET TOOTH

A NIGHT STALKERS ROMANCE STORY

M. L. BUCHMAN

Buchman Bookworks

SIGN UP FOR M. L. BUCHMAN'S NEWSLETTER TODAY

and receive:
Release News
Free Short Stories
a Free book

Get your free book today. Do it now.
free-book.mlbuchman.com

Other works by M. L. Buchman: *(* - also in audio)*

Other works by M. L. Buchman:

Contemporary Romance (cont)

Where Dreams
Where Dreams are Born
Where Dreams Reside
Where Dreams Are of Christmas
Where Dreams Unfold
Where Dreams Are Written

Science Fiction / Fantasy

Deities Anonymous
Cookbook from Hell: Reheated
Saviors 101

Single Titles
The Nara Reaction
Monk's Maze
the Me and Elsie Chronicles

Non-Fiction

Strategies for Success
Managing Your Inner Artist/Writer
Estate Planning for Authors*
Character Voice
Narrate and Record Your Own
Audiobook*

Short Story Series by M. L. Buchman:

Romantic Suspense

Delta Force
Delta Force

Firehawks
The Firehawks Lookouts
The Firehawks Hotshots
The Firebirds

The Night Stalkers
The Night Stalkers
The Night Stalkers 5E
The Night Stalkers CSAR
The Night Stalkers Wedding Stories

US Coast Guard
US Coast Guard

White House Protection Force
White House Protection Force

Contemporary Romance

Eagle Cove
Eagle Cove

Henderson's Ranch
Henderson's Ranch*

Where Dreams
Where Dreams

Thrillers

Dead Chef
Dead Chef

Science Fiction / Fantasy

Deities Anonymous
Deities Anonymous

Other
The Future Night Stalkers
Single Titles

ABOUT THIS BOOK

Helicopter Crew Chief Fiona MacDonald takes her Highland heritage to heart. And when she sees someone break a major pre-battle candy taboo, she lets him have it with saber-sharp disdain.

Del Campbell spent months planning tonight's mission—a hostage rescue from a remote Afghan camp. All goes according to plan, until Fiona catches his bad luck.

Together they can fight the battle. But when the heat fires up between them, can they share the sweetness?

1

"Ye did na just do that."

"Do what?" Del Campbell looked around to try and figure out who was talking to him.

The helicopter's intercom was utterly confusing for conversation unless you knew each person's voice. The fact that it was a woman would make that obvious in any other crew, but not this one. The flight crew aboard the MH-47G twin-rotor Chinook had three women and two men. There were another thirty 75th Rangers in the cargo bay. They were all guys except for the dog handler, but none of them except for the male unit commander were on the intercom anyway.

Somehow, out of all of those people, he suspected that he was indeed the one who had done...whatever it was.

Crew Chief Fi MacDonald came over to where he was plugged into the system. She was a fiery redhead with alabaster skin and green eyes. He had tried to be cool about it throughout the briefing, but with her sitting in the front row it had been hard to look anywhere else.

She flipped off his intercom and then patched her own cable into the console. The roar of the helo's twin turboshaft engines pumping out ten thousand horsepower made conversation near impossible without the headsets.

"You're a freaking idiot, Campbell. Don't you have the common sense God gave a turtle?"

"What are you on about, MacDonald?" Staff Sergeant Fiona MacDonald—hell of an impressive service file. One of the reasons he'd asked for this crew for the mission.

"Tell me you didn't eat the damn thing!"

He looked down at the remains of his dinner. He'd just been sitting here minding his own business. The transit from the USS *Abraham Lincoln* aircraft carrier to Kandahar was going to take three hours and, because it had been his own mission's briefing, he hadn't had time to eat. A Number Five MRE—Chicken Chunks, Meal-Ready-to-Eat—wasn't exactly his idea of fine dining, but it was what he'd grabbed out of the supply box and wolfed down. Only the scraps were left.

Del considered painting the last of the fluorescent yellow cheddar cheese spread on the tip of her nose, but decided that probably wasn't the best way to calm down the helo's crew chief.

"I was hungry. I had dinner. What's the problem?"

"Bloody hell, you are a Campbell, aren't ye? Trying to kill us all just like at Glencoe?"

"The Massacre at Glencoe was over three hundred years ago. I had no part of it."

"Aye, that's a likely story. It was three centuries and a quarter just so you know that no one's forgettin'. You ruddy Campbells slaughtered a whole passel of unarmed MacDonalds, didn't ye?" Her green eyes had a snap and a heat to them that would have fully attested to her having red hair, even if a bit hadn't been peeking out around the edge of her helmet as proof. He wanted to tuck it back in, feel the texture, test if the pale skin was as cool as it looked or fiery with the heat that seemed to radiate from her every pore.

"I was born in Peekskill, New York." And he also knew from her file that despite her wild brogue, she'd been born in Norfolk, Virginia.

"To a bloody Campbell!"

"Dad, yeah. Is there a point to this?" She seemed genuinely upset with him.

She heaved a massive sigh. Even through the Dragonskin armored vest and the survival vest over that, it did things to his imagination. Fi MacDonald had the sort of body that did that to a man no matter how many layers covered it.

He'd also had read that she was a lethal soldier with top marks for keeping her aircraft in the air where it belonged and her crew alive. The only surprise was she was so good that she stood out even in an outfit as elite as the 160th Night Stalkers helicopter regiment.

"My point is, Campbell, you ate the damn candy, didn't ya? Don't be trying to deny it. I seen it plain as day and with me own eyes."

"Yes, I ate the *damn* candy. What of it?"

"Shh! You want to upset the crew? Why do you think I took you out of the intercom circuit?"

He decided against pointing out that his admission had been at a quarter the volume of her accusation.

"So what's the big deal?" He made a point of whispering it.

"Eh?" Damn she was cute. Sparring with her was so much fun.

He repeated it a little louder.

"Well, you've gone and cursed us all, that's what. There's not a soldier in Special Operations who eats the candy in an MRE. That's right bad luck, it is."

"If you aren't supposed to eat it, then why is it in there?"

She shrugged, again tickling his imagination. "Oy, what do I look like? Some kind of chef at Natick Research where they develop these things?"

"No. A gorgeous lunatic maybe."

For some reason, that earned him a smile. As fast as mercury, she switched from irate to dazzling.

"You got a license for that smile?" Because...*Damn!*

"You know, for a Campbell perhaps ye aren't *too* awful."

A gorgeous lunatic. Most people called her Major PIA —pain in the ass. She let them get away with that as long as they saluted when they said it.

License for her smile? From a freaking hot briefing officer from The Activity intelligence agency? She'd take it.

Actually, no, she wouldn't at that. He was just trying to butter her up for some reason.

"You *never* eat the candy, especially not before a mission. Nobody does. Just look." She nodded toward a garbage sack hung on the inside of the hull. It was filled with MRE bags from the Rangers chowing down. And all through the discards there were little flecks of color of unopened candy packets.

"Yes, ma'am. Okay with you if I finish the cheddar cheese?"

"I can let you do that," she offered him a sniff of disdain.

He scooped his finger into the plastic container getting the last bit, then reached out and painted a stripe of it down her nose.

"Goddamn it, Campbell." Her shout was loud enough that several of the Rangers sitting on the hard deck looked up at her. They started laughing when they saw what was going on.

Not deigning to wipe it off just yet, she leaned in close.

"Just don't eat the goddamn candy, Campbell." She knew she was repeating herself, but something about him had thrown her off her game. For one thing, from a single breath away, he smelled as good as he looked: all hot male and competent soldier in his full gear.

"Anything you say, MacDonald."

Which gave her a few other ideas.

She unplugged before she could voice them, turned, then wiped the cheddar off her nose and sucked her finger clean. She made the mistake of glancing back as she returned to her station and saw him watching her with a big smile.

Damn, but he was pretty.

That's what had gotten her in trouble in the first place, watching him while he ate.

It really was too bad he was a Campbell. The blood feud twixt Campbell and MacDonald went back over eight hundred years and she wasn't going to be the one to break it, no matter how impressive the man was.

At the briefing, he'd laid out the intel on the location

of four hostages deep in the no-man's land of Helmand Province. The Taliban were once again on the prowl and this time they'd taken down a Doctors Without Borders team, because who in their right mind wanted their citizens to be healthy after all.

It rapidly became clear, at least to her, that the intel work had been mostly his own. Otherwise he never would have known it so thoroughly. Those four hostages had been worrying everyone for a while, and now he personally had given the best lead yet on where they were stashed.

The rescue mission was going in with four other helos: two DAP Hawk gun platforms and two standard Black Hawks with Delta Force aboard.

Del Campbell could have ridden with Delta, or even in a command seat on one of the DAPs. Instead, he'd geared up with the door-kicking Rangers. That took serious balls and she liked that in a man.

The candy *was* bad luck, but taking the man out for a tussle was a nice prospect even if it was never going to happen. He had raven black hair and even darker eyes, which looked ever so fine on him. Smart, funny, and not willing to back down from one of her tirades. She'd even stretched it a bit just to see, but he'd stood firm.

Then painting her nose with cheddar cheese... That was as fine a declaration of war as any. She couldn't wait.

DEL DID HIS BEST TO STAY OUT OF THE WAY.

The Chinook came in fast and low. It was the only real option.

The terrorist camp had been set on a river-carved mesa. It wasn't high, but the approaches on foot mostly sucked—too easily protected from above. And the area was small enough that parachuting an entire squad in was just asking to have them shot up, because they'd all be piling into just two small landing zones.

The best answer was coming in fast and hot.

So the flight practically scraped its belly up the rocky bight of the Musaqara River then jolted sharply upward to land on the mesa.

The heat came up immediately. Not just the night heat of the Afghan desert that washed aboard the moment the rear ramp was lowered in preparation for landing, but also the heat of protective fire. There were a half dozen sharp thwaps as bullets hit the Chinook's hull and made it ring while the Rangers were storming down the ramp.

Then the DAP Hawks kicked in from high above. Hard buzz-saw bursts from their M134 Miniguns, chewing up the opposition. Suddenly the bad guys on the ground had something a lot more important to worry about than their Chinook.

At least until the Rangers took up positions around the camp, joining the firefight from a new angle. Then they had multiple things to worry about.

Del was combat qualified and he'd thought about stepping out with the Rangers, but he could see by the way they moved just how good they were. He'd screw up their highly coordinated actions if he tried to join in.

"All dressed up and nowhere to go," he muttered to himself as the helo lifted away to hide once more in the darkness, taking with it his last chance to join the Rangers. It had been completely his mission, right up to this instant and now he didn't know what to do with himself.

"Try wearin' a kilt next time." Fi MacDonald over the intercom from her position at the port side gun emplacement. He certainly had that voice down after her tirade. He took a moment to appreciate the image of her out of all that battle gear and dancing in a proper tartan dress.

"If you will, I will." It would be worth the price. "Bet you got great legs."

"And a great ass too. Not that you'll ever see it. How are your legs, me fine lad?"

Another spate of gunfire somehow found the

Chinook, rattling down the side of the hull—pure chance.

There was a grunt and a sharp curse from Fi.

Del hurried up the length of the cargo bay.

Fi was sitting on the deck, wrapping a piece of duct tape around the leg of her flightsuit.

"Hell of a bandage there, MacDonald."

"How come you're the one who ate the candy and *I'm* the one who gets shot?"

"Shot?" A voice sounded over the intercom. "Report!"

"Meat shot, through and through on the thigh and the arm. No arterial. Just stings like a couple of jabs from an Englishman's lance."

"Roger," and the pilot was gone. Del supposed he had other things to worry about.

He helped her tape over her arm and she hissed at the pain. Fi began hauling herself to her feet, very unsuccessfully.

"Just sit."

"Gotta man the gun."

The Chinook didn't carry much armament. Two M134 miniguns, one out either side, and an FN M240 machine gun on the rear ramp. A twin-rotor Chinook was a heavy mover—the DAP Hawks were the serious gun platforms. But having so little, the Chinook needed all of the defense it could get.

"One-handed and one-legged? You and Ahab. I can do that."

Fi just looked at him. "That's a minigun, Campbell."

"Shot them before, MacDonald."

"Any idea what to shoot at?"

That was a problem. He knew the camp's layout so well that it could be tattooed on the inside of his eyelids. But the tactics of the ground troops, that he didn't know well enough.

"Help me up, goddamn it."

"Your arm can't handle the gun." She was holding it tightly against her chest. He wondered if there was a fractured bone under that tape.

"My eyes still work. I'll say where, you aim and fire. And don't bloody miss. The M134 could make the Massacre at Glencoe look like a May Day picnic."

He got her to her feet. She hung onto him with her good hand. They were close enough to the same height, that if they moved their helmets until they were almost touching, they could see out the same window around the gun.

"We're going to start at the edge of camp until you have a feel for it, Campbell."

"Just tell me where to hit."

4

THE LAST CAME OUT AS A SNARL.

Fi could get to like this Del Campbell despite his last name. Attitude and lots of it—the kind that came from raw masses of competence.

She tried to wipe at the sweat stinging her eyes with her free hand, which hurt like hell. She definitely wouldn't do that again. At a loss for what else to do, she tipped her head down and wiped her eyes on the point of his shoulder blade.

Strong, solid. It would be a fine place to tuck in on a cold winter's night. But for the moment—

She flipped down her night-vision goggles with a sharp nod, and studied the battle below.

"There! At the southwest corner behind the shed. You've got a leak." Out the back corner of the camp, Talis were doing what Talis always did—running away to fight another day. The Taliban leaders were always squeezing out the backs of villages and leaving the local recruits to do the dying.

Not today.

Del grabbed the Minigun's dual handles. A yank on the trigger and the motor-driven six barrels of the Gatling gun spun up to five hundred RPM and fifty rounds a second drove down out of the sky. Every fifth round was a tracer, bright green in their NVGs.

Like a good boy, Del started the gun high, striking a line in the dirt beyond the camp and in front of the escaping Talis. Then he painted his way back toward them in a fast back-and-forth lashing until he drove them under.

"You were slow on the trigger release. They were already dead, conserve your ammo. The painting was good, but use shorter strokes. Next..."

They worked their way around the camp as the other two gunships did the same. The Rangers and Delta had small reflective tabs on their shoulders that glowed under the infrared searchlight shining down from one of the DAP Hawks.

They couldn't shoot at any of the buildings until they were sure where the hostages were being held.

But they didn't lack for targets.

The synchronicity that built up between them went from testing to smooth to downright awesome. They got into a groove so true and deep that they could have launched a rocket sled right down it.

A slight twist where her hand clenched his shoulder —another leak plugged.

This time with a three-second burst instead of eleven. Her hip pushed against his and he swung the gun to a completely new angle of attack and took out a stubborn gun emplacement and part of the Talis' motor pool. Another squeeze of her hand and the rest of the motor pool disappeared.

It was dreamy.

Hard to concentrate.

So aware of the connection between them that she wasn't conscious of being separate. What would it be like to make love with such a man, with such a synchronicity between them?

The Delta Force operators suddenly rushed out of a building. There were four infrared hotspots in their midst, but with no reflective indicators on their shoulders.

The hostages?

Del's heartfelt, "Yes!" told her it was.

She tried to join in, but couldn't seem to find her voice. She wondered briefly where she'd left it, but couldn't imagine.

The Chinook and one of the Black Hawks plunged back to the ground. Rangers piled aboard in a swirl of gunpowder-scented desert dust. In moments, they were aloft again, racing downriver.

She saw the bright sizzle of Hellfire missiles striking down from the DAP Hawks to obliterate the camp. But she didn't see the missiles land.

Too bad, she always liked a good fireworks show.

5

Del caught her as Fi slid bonelessly to deck.

"Medic!"

"She got a pulse?" a man with bloody hands clutching white bandages called out.

He checked. "Feels strong. For now."

"Okay, give me a minute."

Del began checking her over. He only had the basic medical training given to any grunt, basically a CPR course plus morphine.

He eased off her helmet and ran his hands through her hair. It was even thicker than he'd imagined. When he checked his hands, they weren't covered in the red of blood, though they'd just been buried in the red of her hair.

It was hard to tell in the dim cabin light, but her face looked even paler than before. A hand on her cheek told him it was so soft that it seemed impossible. And cool, but not cold...yet.

The releases on her survival vest got him down to her bulletproof Dragonskin.

He slipped his hands under her vest: down her back, up her sides, and over her belly. Still no blood. And there were certain places he was just going to trust to the vest. Both arms clean, except for some smears around the duct tape bandage he'd placed there.

Both legs the same.

Once more he rolled her over enough to reach behind her.

One cheek, nothing. The other...his hand came away wet and dark red.

Someone had shot Fiona MacDonald in the ass.

He'd bet a thousand dollars that she was going to be some kind of pissed.

If she made it.

6

"Who let you in here?" Fi tried to imagine if she'd ever been so happy to see anyone.

"Got a complaint at the front. Something about a whiny Scotsman and they aren't going to treat any such unless I can get her to behave like an actual human being."

"Scots*woman*. And I'm fine. Get me out of this joint, Campbell." Actually, she'd been awake about thirty seconds and was freaking out because she had no idea where the hell she was. It was dim and incredibly loud.

"Sure," he smiled down at her. "Just watch the first step; it's a doozy."

He slid his hand into hers and she clamped down on it hard. It reminded her of how good it had felt to lean against him during the battle. How in harmony every thought, every motion had been. She'd never found a man like that, even after months together—never mind the first few hours. Or had it been minutes? It all blurred together.

Fiona looked around as her world came back into focus. The belly of a C-130 cargo plane. At least that explained the roaring noise. The Hercs were notoriously uninsulated against the noise of the four Allison T56 turboprops.

She was on the lower level of a two-tier rack of hospital stretchers.

"Why am I strapped in?" Not that she felt much like sitting up.

"They're called seatbelts, MacDonald. Get used to it. We're five more hours to home."

Five hours to home. That meant that she'd been out of it for at least twelve hours, more likely eighteen. That was scary close to the big bad darkness. She held his hand tighter to keep the BBD at bay.

She managed to raise her head. Six racks of two stretchers each. Over to the other side were four people in civilian clothes sitting in web seats mounted along the side of the hull.

"Yep," Del noticed the direction she was looking. "Got all four hostages out and no fatalities. You know, after four months of captivity, the first thing they did was help patch up the guys who got them out."

"And gal."

"Actually, that was me and one of the Rangers. Hope you don't mind me saying, but you have an amazing behind Staff Sergeant Fiona MacDonald. Totally first class, even if there is a new hole in one cheek."

"You ate the candy...and *I'm* the one who got a hole shot in my butt?"

"Arm and leg too, but yeah."

"Goddamn you and your foul luck, Campbell." Though she didn't let go of his hand.

"I consider it good luck."

"How's that?"

"Can think of at least four reasons. One, we saved the hostages. Two, we're both alive."

Fi considered how else this could have ended up. A round through the hip instead of her butt could have had massive nerve damage. Two inches higher on the arm and she'd have no elbow. A few centimeters to the either side on her leg and she'd have pumped enough arterial blood out that she'd be making this trip in a box instead of on a stretcher.

"And three, you saw my butt."

Del just grinned. "Cutting your pants off was just one of the joys of this day."

"It's amazing what a lowlife Campbell will do to get a gander at a lady's behind."

His snort of laughter when she said "lady" he'd be paying for later.

"Tell me the last one."

"Well, that's the best luck ever. I got to meet you."

When he leaned down and kissed her, she decided that she'd have to agree. Best luck ever.

Though next time?

She'd eat the candy and *he* could be the one shot in the butt.

———

*If you enjoyed this, keep reading for an excerpt from a book
you're going to love.*
...and a review is always welcome (it really helps)...

**IF YOU ENJOYED THIS, YOU'LL LOVE
THE NIGHT STALKERS 5E**

TARGET OF THE HEART (EXCERPT)

Major Pete Napier hovered his MH-47G Chinook helicopter ten kilometers outside of Lhasa, Tibet and a mere two inches off the tundra. A mixed action team of Delta Force and The Activity—the slipperiest intel group on the planet—flung themselves aboard.

The additional load sent an infinitesimal shift in the cyclic control in his right hand. The hydraulics to close the rear loading ramp hummed through the entire frame of the massive helicopter. By the time his crew chief could reach forward to slap an "all secure" signal against his shoulder, they were already ten feet up and fifty out. That was enough altitude. He kept the nose down as he clawed for speed in the thin air at eleven thousand feet.

"Totally worth it," one of the D-boys announced as soon as he was on the Chinook's internal intercom.

He'd have to remember to tell that to the two Black Hawks flying guard for him...when they were in a friendly country and could risk a radio transmission. This deep inside China—or rather Chinese-held territory as the CIA's mission-briefing spook had insisted on calling it —radios attracted attention and were only used to avoid imminent death and destruction.

"Great, now I just need to get us out of this alive."

"Do that, Pete. We'd appreciate it."

He wished to hell he had a stealth bird like the one that had gone into bin Laden's compound. But the one that had crashed during that raid had been blown up. Where there was one, there were always two, but the second had gone back into hiding as thoroughly as if it had never existed. He hadn't heard a word about it since.

The Tibetan terrain was amazing, even if all he could see of it was the monochromatic green of night vision. And blackness. The largest city in Tibet lay a mere ten kilometers away and they were flying over barren wilderness. He could crash out here and no one would know for decades unless some yak herder stumbled upon them. Or were yaks in Mongolia? He was a corn-fed, white boy from Colorado, what did he know about Tibet? Most of the countries he'd flown into on Black Ops missions he'd only seen at night anyway.

While moving very, very fast.

Like now.

The inside of his visor was painted with overlapping readouts. A pre-defined terrain map, the best that modern satellite imaging could build made the first layer. This wasn't some crappy, on-line, look-at-a-picture-of-your-house display. Someone had a pile of dung outside their goat pen? He could see it, tell you how high it was, and probably say if they were pygmy goats or full-size

LaManchas by the size of their shit-pellets if he zoomed in.

On top of that were projected the forward-looking infrared camera images. The FLIR imaging gave him a real-time overlay, in case someone had put an addition onto their goat shed since the last satellite pass or parked their tractor across his intended flight path.

His nervous system was paying autonomic attention to that combined landscape. He also compensated for the thin air at altitude as he instinctively chose when to start his climb over said goat shed or his swerve around it.

It was the third layer, the tactical display that had most of his attention. At least he and the two Black Hawks flying escort on him were finally on the move.

To insert this deep into Tibet, without passing over Bhutan or Nepal, they'd had to add wingtanks on the Black Hawks' hardpoints where he'd much rather have a couple banks of Hellfire missiles. Still, they had 20 mm chain guns and the crew chiefs had miniguns which was some comfort. His twin-rotor Chinook might be the biggest helicopter that the Night Stalkers flew, but it was the cargo van of Special Operations and only had two miniguns and a machine gun of its own. Though he'd put his three crew chiefs up against the best Black Hawk shooter any day.

While the action team was busy infiltrating the capital city and gathering intelligence on the particularly brutal Chinese assistant administrator, Pete and his crews had been squatting out in the wilderness under a camouflage net designed to make his helo look like just another god-forsaken Himalayan lump of granite.

Command had determined that it was better for the helos to wait on site through the day than risk flying out and back in. He and his crew had stood shifts on guard duty, but none of them had slept. They'd been flying together too long to have any new jokes, so they'd played a lot of cribbage. He'd long ago ruled no gambling on a mission, after a fistfight had broken out about a bluff hand that cost a Marine three hundred and forty-seven dollars. Marines hated losing to Army no matter how many times it happened. They'd had to sit on him for a long time before he calmed down.

Tonight's mission was part of an on-going campaign to discredit the Chinese "presence" in Tibet on the international stage—as if occupying the country the last sixty-plus years didn't count toward ruling, whether invited or not. As usual, there was a crucial vote coming up at the U.N.—that, as usual, the Chinese could be guaranteed to ignore. However, the ever-hopeful CIA was in a hurry to make sure that any damaging information that they could validate was disseminated as thoroughly as possible prior to the vote.

Not his concern.

His concern was, were they going to pass over some Chinese sentry post at their top speed of a hundred and ninety-six miles an hour? The sentries would then call down a couple Shenyang J-16 jet fighters that could hustle along at Mach 2—over fifteen *hundred* mph—to fry his sorry ass. He knew there was a pair of them parked at Lhasa along with some older gear that would be just as effective against his three helos.

"Don't suppose you could get a move on, Pete?"

"Eat shit, Nicolai!" He was a good man to have as a copilot. Pete knew he was holding on too tight, and Nicolai knew that a joke was the right way to ease the moment.

He, Nicolai, and the four pilots in the two Black Hawks had a long way to go tonight and he'd never make it if he stayed so tight on the controls that he could barely maneuver. Pete eased off and felt his fingers tingle with the rush of returning blood. They dove down into gorges and followed them as long as they dared. They hugged cliff walls at every opportunity to decrease their radar profile. And they climbed.

That was the true danger—they would be up near the helos' limits when they crossed over the backbone of the Himalayas in their rush for India. The air was so rarefied that they burned fuel at a prodigious rate. Their reserve didn't allow for any extended battles while crossing the border...not for any battle at all really.

———

It was pitch dark outside her helicopter when Captain Danielle Delacroix stamped on the left rudder pedal while giving the big Chinook right-directed control on the cyclic. It tipped her most of the way onto her side but let her continue in a straight line. A Chinook's rotors were sixty feet across—front to back they overlapped to make the spread a hundred feet long. By cross-controlling her bird to tip it, she managed to execute a straight line between two mock pylons only thirty feet apart. They were made of thin cloth so they wouldn't down the helo if you sliced one—she was the only trainee to not have cut one yet.

At her current angle of attack, she took up less than a half-rotor of width, just twenty-four feet. That left her nearly three feet to either side, sufficient as she was moving at under a hundred knots.

The training instructor sitting beside her in the copilot's seat didn't react as she swooped through the training course at Fort Campbell, Kentucky. Only child of a single mother, she was used to providing her own feedback loops, so she didn't expect anything else. Those who expected outside validation rarely survived the SOAR induction testing, never mind the two years of training that followed.

As a loner kid, Danielle had learned that self-motivated congratulations and fun were much easier to come by than external ones. She'd spent innumerable hours deep in her mind as a pre-teen superheroine. At twenty-nine she was well on her way to becoming a real life one, though Helo-girl had never been a character she'd thought of in her youth.

External validation or not, after two years of training with the U.S. Army's 160th Special Operations Aviation Regiment she was ready for some action. At least *she* was convinced that she was. But the trainers of Fort Campbell, Kentucky had not signed off on anyone in her trainee class yet. Nor had they given any hint of when they might.

She ducked ten tons of racing Chinook under a bridge and bounced into a near vertical climb to clear the power line on the far side. Like a ride on the toboggan at

Terrassee Dufferin during *Le Carnaval de Québec,* only with ten thousand horsepower at her fingertips. Using her Army signing bonus—the first money in her life that was truly hers—to attend *Le Carnaval* had been her one trip back to her birthplace since her mother took them to America when she was ten.

To even apply to SOAR required five years of prior military rotorcraft experience. She had applied after seven years because of a chance encounter—or rather what she'd thought was a chance encounter at the time.

Captain Justin Roberts had been a top Chinook pilot, the one who had convinced her to switch from her beloved Black Hawk and try out the massive twin-rotor craft. One flight and she'd been a goner, begging her commander until he gave in and let her cross over to the new platform. Justin had made the jump from the 10th Mountain Division to the 160th SOAR not long after that.

Then one night she'd been having pizza in Watertown, New York a couple miles off the 10th's base at Fort Drum.

"Danielle?" Justin had greeted her with the surprise of finding a good friend in an unexpected place. Danielle had always liked Justin—even if he was a too-tall, too-handsome cowboy and completely knew it. But "good friend" was unusual for Danielle, with anyone, and Justin came close.

"Captain Roberts," as a dry greeting over the top edge of her Suzanne Brockmann novel didn't faze him in the slightest.

"Mind if I join ya?" A question he then answered for himself by sliding into the opposite seat and taking a slice of her pizza. She been thinking of taking the leftovers back to base, but that was now an idle thought.

"Are you enjoying life in SOAR?" she did her best to appear a normal, social human, a skill she'd learned by rote. *Greeting someone you knew after a time apart? Ask a question about them.* "They treating you well?"

"Whoo-ee, you have no idea, Danielle," his voice was smooth as...well, always...so she wouldn't think about it also sounding like a pickup line. He was beautiful but didn't interest her; the outgoing ones never did.

"Tell me." *Men love to talk about themselves, so let them.*

And he did. But she'd soon forgotten about her novel and would have forgotten the pizza if he hadn't reminded her to eat.

His stories shifted from intriguing to fascinating. There was a world out there that she'd been only peripherally aware of. The Night Stalkers of the 160th SOAR weren't simply better helicopter pilots, they were the most highly-trained and best-equipped ones anywhere. Their missions were pure razor's edge and Black Op dark.

He'd left her with a hundred questions and enough interest to fill out an application to the 160th Special Operations Aviation Regiment (airborne). Being a decent guy, Justin even paid for the pizza after eating half.

The speed at which she was rushed into testing told her that her meeting with Justin hadn't been by chance and that she owed him more than half a pizza next time they met. She'd asked after him a couple of times since she'd made it past the qualification exams—and the examiners' brutal interviews that had left her questioning her sanity, never mind her ability.

"Justin Roberts is presently deployed, ma'am," was the only response she'd ever gotten.

Now that she was through training—almost, had to be soon, didn't it?—Danielle realized that was probably less of an evasion and more likely to do with the brutal op tempo the Night Stalkers maintained. The SOAR 1st Battalion had just won the coveted Lt. General Ellis D. Parker awards for Outstanding Combat Aviation Battalion *and* Aviation Battalion of the Year. They'd been on deployment every single day of the last year, actually of the last decade-plus since 9/11.

The very first Special Forces boots on the ground in Afghanistan were delivered that October by the Night Stalkers and nothing had slacked off since. Justin might be in the 5th battalion D company, but they were just as heavily assigned as the 1st.

Part of the recruits' training had included tours in Afghanistan. But unlike their prior deployments, these were brief, intense, and then they'd be back in the States pushing to integrate their new skills.

SOAR needed her training to end and so did she.

Danielle was ready for the job, in her own, inestimable opinion. But she wasn't going to get there until the trainers signed off that she'd reached fully mission-qualified proficiency. FMQ was the gold star of the Night Stalkers pipeline.

The Fort Campbell training course was never set up the same from one flight to the next, but it always had a time limit. The time would be short and they didn't tell you what it was. So she drove the Chinook for all it was worth like Regina Jaquess waterskiing her way to U.S. Ski Team Female Athlete of the Year.

The Night Stalkers were a damned secretive lot, and after two years of training, she understood why. With seven years flying for the 10th, she'd thought she was good.

She'd been repeatedly lauded as one of the top pilots at Fort Drum.

The Night Stalkers had offered an education in what it really meant to fly. In the two years of training, she'd flown more hours than in the seven years prior, despite two deployments to Iraq. And spent more time in the classroom than her life-to-date accumulated flight hours.

But she was ready now. It was *très viscérale,* right down in her bones she could feel it. The Chinook was as much a part of her nervous system as breathing.

Too bad they didn't build men the way they built the big Chinooks—especially the MH-47G which were built specifically to SOAR's requirements. The aircraft were steady, trustworthy, and the most immensely powerful helicopters deployed in the U.S. Army—what more could a girl ask for? But finding a superhero man to go with her superhero helicopter was just a fantasy for a lonely girl who'd once had dreams of more.

She dove down into a canyon and slid to a hover mere inches over the reservoir inside the thirty-second window laid out on the flight plan.

Danielle resisted a sigh. She was ready for something to happen and to happen soon.

PETE'S CHINOOK AND HIS TWO ESCORT BLACK HAWKS crossed into the mountainous province of Sikkim, India ten feet over the glaciers and still moving fast. It was an hour before dawn, they'd made it out of China while it was still dark.

"Thirty minutes of fuel remaining," Nicolai said it like a personal challenge when they hit the border.

"Thanks, I never would have noticed."

It had been a nail-biting tradeoff: the more fuel he burned, the more easily he climbed due to the lighter load. The more he climbed, the faster he burned what little fuel remained.

Safe in Indian airspace he climbed hard as Nicolai counted down the minutes remaining, burning fuel even faster than he had been while crossing the mountains of southern Tibet. They caught up with the U.S. Air Force HC-130P Combat King refueling tanker with only ten minutes of fuel left.

"Ram that bitch," Nicolai called out.

Pete extended the refueling probe which reached only a few feet beyond the forward edge of the rotor blade and drove at the basket trailing behind the tanker on its long hose.

He nailed it on the first try despite the fluky winds. Striking the valve in the basket with over four hundred pounds of pressure, a clamp snapped over the refueling probe and Jet A fuel shot into his tanks.

His helo had the least fuel due to having the most men aboard, so he was first in line. His Number Two picked up the second refueling basket trailing off the other wing of the Combat King. Thirty seconds and three hundred gallons later and he was breathing much more easily.

"Ah," Nicolai sighed. "It is better than the sex," his thick Russian accent only ever surfaced in this moment or in a bar while picking up women.

"Hey, Nicolai," Nicky the Greek called over the intercom from his crew chief position seated behind Pete. "Do you make love in Russian?"

A question Pete had always been careful to avoid.

"For you, I make special exception." That got a laugh over the system.

Which explained why Pete always kept his mouth shut at this moment.

"The ladies, Nicolai? What about the ladies?" Alfie the portside gunner asked.

"Ah," he sighed happily as he signaled that the other helos had finished their refueling and formed up to either side, "the ladies love the Russian. They don't need to know I grew up in Maryland and I learn my great-great-grandfather's native tongue at the University called Virginia."

He sounded so pleased that Pete wished he'd done the same rather than study Japanese and Mandarin.

Another two hours of—Thank God—straight-and-level flight at altitude through the breaking dawn and they landed on the aircraft carrier awaiting them in the Bay of Bengal. India had agreed to turn a blind eye as long as the Americans never actually touched their soil.

Once standing on the deck—and the worst of the

kinks had been worked out—he pulled his team together: six pilots and seven crew chiefs.

"Honor to serve!" He saluted them sharply.

"Hell yeah!" They shouted in unison and saluted in turn. It was their version of spiking the football in the end zone.

A petty officer in a bright green vest appeared at his elbow, "Follow me please, sir." He pointed toward the Navy-gray command structure that towered above the carrier's deck. The rear admiral of the entire carrier strike group was waiting for him just outside the entrance. Not a good idea to keep a one-star waiting, so he waved at the team.

"See you in the mess for dinner," he shouted to the crew over the noise of an F-18 Hornet fighter jet trapping on the #2 wire. After two days of surviving on MREs while squatting on the Tibetan tundra, he was ready for a steak, a burger, a mountain of pasta, whatever. Or maybe all three.

The green escorted him across the hazards of the busy flight deck. Pete had kept his helmet on to buffer the noise, but even at that he winced as another Hornet fired up and was flung aloft by the catapult.

"Orders, Major Napier," the Rear Admiral handed him a folded sheet the moment he arrived. "Hate to lose you." He saluted, which Pete automatically returned before looking down at the sheet of paper in his hands. The man was gone before the import of Pete's orders slammed in.

A different green-clad deckhand showed up with Pete's duffle bag and began guiding him toward a loading

C-2 Greyhound twin-prop airplane. It was parked
Number Two for the launch catapult, close behind the
raised jet-blast deflector.

His crew, being led across in the opposite direction to
return to the berthing decks below, looked at him aghast.

"Stateside," was all he managed to gasp out as they
passed.

A stream of foul cursing followed him from behind.
Their crew was tight. Why the hell was Command
breaking it up?

And what in the name of fuck-all had he done to
deserve this?

He glanced at the orders again as he stumbled up the
Greyhound's rear ramp and crash landed into a seat.

Training rookies?

It was worse than a demotion.

This was punishment.

———

Keep reading at fine retailers everywhere.
Target of the Heart
...and don't forget that review. It really helps me out.

ABOUT THE AUTHOR

M.L. Buchman started the first of over 60 novels, 100 short stories, and a fast-growing pile of audiobooks while flying from South Korea to ride his bicycle across the Australian Outback. Part of a solo around the world trip that ultimately launched his writing career in: thrillers, military romantic suspense, contemporary romance, and SF/F.

Recently named in *The 20 Best Romantic Suspense Novels: Modern Masterpieces* by ALA's Booklist, they have also selected his works three times as "Top-10 Romance Novel of the Year." NPR and B&N listed other works as "Best 5 of the Year."

As a 30-year project manager with a geophysics degree who has: designed and built houses, flown and jumped out of planes, and solo-sailed a 50' ketch, he is awed by what's possible. More at: www.mlbuchman.com.

Other works by M. L. Buchman: (* - also in audio)

Thrillers

Dead Chef
Swap Out!
One Chef!
Two Chef!

Miranda Chase
Drone*
Thunderbolt*
Condor*

Romantic Suspense

Delta Force
Target Engaged*
Heart Strike*
Wild Justice*
Midnight Trust*

Firehawks
MAIN FLIGHT
Pure Heat
Full Blaze
Hot Point*
Flash of Fire*
Wild Fire
SMOKEJUMPERS
Wildfire at Dawn*
Wildfire at Larch Creek*
Wildfire on the Skagit*

The Night Stalkers
MAIN FLIGHT
The Night Is Mine
I Own the Dawn
Wait Until Dark
Take Over at Midnight
Light Up the Night
Bring On the Dusk
By Break of Day

AND THE NAVY
Christmas at Steel Beach
Christmas at Peleliu Cove
WHITE HOUSE HOLIDAY
Daniel's Christmas*
Frank's Independence Day*
Peter's Christmas*
Zachary's Christmas*
Roy's Independence Day*
Damien's Christmas*
5E
Target of the Heart
Target Lock on Love
Target of Mine
Target of One's Own

Shadow Force: Psi
At the Slightest Sound*
At the Quietest Word*

White House Protection Force
Off the Leash*
On Your Mark*
In the Weeds*

Contemporary Romance

Eagle Cove
Return to Eagle Cove
Recipe for Eagle Cove
Longing for Eagle Cove
Keepsake for Eagle Cove

Henderson's Ranch
Nathan's Big Sky*
Big Sky, Loyal Heart*
Big Sky Dog Whisperer*

Love Abroad
Heart of the Cotswolds: England
Path of Love: Cinque Terre, Italy

Other works by M. L. Buchman:

Contemporary Romance (cont)

Where Dreams
Where Dreams are Born
Where Dreams Reside
Where Dreams Are of Christmas
Where Dreams Unfold
Where Dreams Are Written

Science Fiction / Fantasy

Deities Anonymous
Cookbook from Hell: Reheated
Saviors 101

Single Titles
The Nara Reaction
Monk's Maze
the Me and Elsie Chronicles

Non-Fiction

Strategies for Success
Managing Your Inner Artist/Writer
Estate Planning for Authors*
Character Voice
Narrate and Record Your Own Audiobook*

Short Story Series by M. L. Buchman:

Romantic Suspense

Delta Force
Delta Force

Firehawks
The Firehawks Lookouts
The Firehawks Hotshots
The Firebirds

The Night Stalkers
The Night Stalkers
The Night Stalkers 5E
The Night Stalkers CSAR
The Night Stalkers Wedding Stories

US Coast Guard
US Coast Guard

White House Protection Force
White House Protection Force

Contemporary Romance

Eagle Cove
Eagle Cove

Henderson's Ranch
Henderson's Ranch*

Where Dreams
Where Dreams

Thrillers

Dead Chef
Dead Chef

Science Fiction / Fantasy

Deities Anonymous
Deities Anonymous

Other
The Future Night Stalkers
Single Titles

SIGN UP FOR M. L. BUCHMAN'S NEWSLETTER TODAY

and receive:
Release News
Free Short Stories
a Free Book

Get your free book today. Do it now.
free-book.mlbuchman.com